The Twelve Dancing Princesses

THE CLASSIC
FAIRY TALE COLLECTION

The Twelve Dancing Princesses

Retold by JOHN CECH

Illustrated by LUCY CORVINO

STERLING

New York / London

ONCE there was a land where the cobblers were always busy. Their days were spent making new shoes for the kingdom's twelve beautiful princesses. Each day they brought twelve new pairs of shoes to the palace, but by the next morning the shoes were completely worn out.

The king tugged on his beard when he saw the bills that the cobblers presented for the new shoes. One day he asked his daughters, "How can you each wear out a pair of shoes every day?"

The princesses looked knowingly at one another. "Dear Papa," one of his daughters replied, "you know how busy we are. Why, we spend all day dashing from one side of the castle to the other. Even the sturdiest shoes would wear out."

But the king knew there must be another explanation. His daughters' shoes were just fine at dinner each evening, but by morning they looked like they had walked up and down a range of mountains. And so the king decreed throughout his realm that whoever could discover the secret of his daughters' worn-out shoes would have his choice of the princesses for a bride.

Young men from around the country gathered to try their luck, but none could find the truth.

After months of failure, the king made the prize even greater. Whoever solved this mystery, he declared, would not only marry the princess of his choice but would also become the next king.

While this mystery was unfolding at the castle, a soldier was trudging through the woods of the kingdom, returning from years of battles and hardship far away. He had just stopped to rest on a log when, out of the dim depths of the forest, an old woman appeared and sat down next to him. She, too, was weary from walking.

"Can you spare a little water and a crust of bread?" she asked the soldier.

"Of course, Granny," the soldier replied, and gave her half of his loaf, then poured her a cup of water from his canteen.

When they had eaten their lunch, the old woman asked the soldier where he was going, and he replied that he didn't know. He was simply following the path through the woods and hoping it would lead him somewhere.

"Well, son," the old woman replied, "if you take the fork in the road to the right, it will bring you to the king's castle." She told the soldier all about the twelve princesses, their worn-out shoes, the king's offer, and those who had already tried and failed. "Maybe you can solve the riddle that's got everyone scratching their heads."

"But how can I succeed when so many others have not?" he asked.

"Ah, you must remember only one thing: no matter what you do, do not accept anything to drink from the princesses. Not water, not cider, not even hot milk. Nothing."

Then she took the cloak she was carrying and placed it in his hands.

"Oh, Granny. I can't accept this cloak from you. The nights are still cold, and you will need it," the soldier said.

"No, my son, take it," she insisted. "This cloak will make you invisible. You are the one who will need it. You'll see."

The soldier looked down at the carefully folded fabric. When he looked up, the old woman had vanished into the woods.

Strange, he thought. But he tucked the cloak into his pack and made his way through the woods and on to the palace.

When he arrived at last, the soldier presented himself to the king and asked for a chance to solve the mystery of the princesses' shoes.

"Of course," the king agreed. But he thought to himself, *this fellow doesn't stand a chance. The princesses will lead him on a merry chase.*

The soldier was shown to a cot in the hall just outside the princesses' chamber. When they came up to bed for the evening, the eldest princess gave the soldier a cup of fragrant tea.

"This will help you to stay up," she said with kindness and a warm smile. Then she disappeared into her bedroom, closing the door behind her.

The princesses are very beautiful, the soldier thought, *and they're so considerate.* He sat down to rest and was about to sip the tea when he remembered the old woman's words. Recalling her warning, he poured the tea into his canteen, laid down on the cot, and pretended to be fast asleep, snoring like a bear in a cave. And he waited.

When midnight struck on the tower clock, the door to the princesses' bedroom cracked open, and the youngest princess looked out into the hallway. Seeing the empty teacup—which had held the sleeping potion—she whispered to her sisters, "Come on! He's asleep."

The twelve sisters tiptoed out the door of their chamber. They were dressed in lovely, flowing ball gowns. The sparkling new shoes on their feet were soundless on the flagstones of the dark hallway. As soon as the princesses were out of sight, the soldier quickly pulled the cloak from his pack, took off his boots so he wouldn't make any noise, and hurried behind them down the long corridor. He could see the sisters' candles flickering in the distance, and soon caught up with them as they went down, down, down into the depths of the castle.

The old woman had been right. The cloak did make him invisible, and he got so close to the last princess—the youngest of the twelve— that he nearly bumped into her when the sisters suddenly stopped their downward climb. Just in front of them lay a large lake, glistening beneath the castle. The edge of the soldier's cloak ever so slightly touched one of the princess's fingers.

"Sisters, I think someone is following us," the youngest princess said with alarm. They all turned to look behind them, but they could see no one, so the eldest sister told her that she must be imagining things.

"Hurry," she said, "or we will miss the start of the dance."

Ah, well, that explains it! the soldier thought to himself. *They go dancing—and in the middle of the night!*

The sisters made their way to the edge of the lake, passing through three lanes of trees that arched over the path. The first group of trees had leaves made of silver.

Hmmm, thought the soldier, *I'd better take back some evidence for the king*. And he broke off a small stem of leaves from one of the trees. The little branch made a popping sound when the soldier snapped it.

"What was that!" the youngest princess exclaimed. "I just know we're being followed."

"Oh, that is just the princes making noise in their boats. They're calling for us," the eldest sister replied.

The leaves on the next group of trees were all made of gold. The soldier snapped off one of these branches, too. It popped like the silver one had.

"There's that sound again," the youngest sister cried.

"Oh, it's just the leaves crackling as we walk by," the eldest princess chided.

The last grove of trees had leaves made of diamonds, and as the soldier took one of these, it snapped louder than the others.

"Did you hear THAT?" the youngest princess exclaimed again. "Now I'm sure there's someone behind us!"

"It's only the sound of the oars in the water," said the eldest princess. "Look, we're nearly there."

Twelve boats were drawn up to the shore of the lake, each with a prince inside to row the princesses across the water. In the distance, a castle was lit up. The sounds of musicians tuning their instruments drifted across the still surface of the lake. The soldier carefully hid himself in the boat carrying the youngest princess, while the young prince strained at the oars to keep up with the other boats.

"This boat seems so heavy tonight," said the prince. "We must be rowing into the wind." Even though his arms ached, the thought of the evening ahead kept him rowing.

When all the boats had landed, the princes and princesses ran up the hill to the castle, where the music for the dance had just begun. The soldier followed a short distance behind, so as not to accidentally step on the hems of any ball gowns. The music was so entrancing that he joined the dance, too, twirling each of the princesses when he had the chance.

"Sister," the youngest princess whispered. "There's something strange going on tonight."

"I know," her elder sister replied. "Something was lifting me up, and I was dancing in the air!"

As dawn came and the princesses prepared to leave, the soldier followed them back to their boats. This time he rode across the lake with the eldest princess, since her boat was the first to leave. When they reached the opposite shore, he ran ahead, through the trees and up the passageway, back to his place outside their room. He took off his magic cloak, lay down under the covers, and began to snore like a hive of bees.

When the princesses arrived, they found their soldier fast asleep. They smiled at one another, took off their shoes and left them in a pile outside their bedroom door, and then went to bed, yawning.

What an amazing night, the soldier thought as he drifted off to sleep himself.

In the morning, the soldier prepared to tell the king all about the events of the night before. But then he thought, *the king has given me three nights. Let's see if the princesses do the same thing. Besides, I have not had such fun in a long, long time.*

And so the soldier followed the princesses again, just as he had done the previous evening. This time, he tucked into his pocket one of the napkins, embroidered with threads of silk and gold, which came with the refreshments that were served at the ball.

On the third night, he followed them once more, through the trees and across the lake to the dance. Before he left, he took a golden cup from the table. And again he lay snoring blissfully when the princesses returned and left their worn-out shoes outside their bedroom door.

On the third morning, the king summoned the soldier to the throne room.

"Well?" demanded the king. "Have you solved the mystery? I see that my daughters continue to wear their shoes to smithereens."

"Yes, your majesty," replied the soldier. "I have. The princesses go dancing every night."

"But where?" the king asked. "We haven't held a ball in the kingdom for many years. Not since my dear queen died. She loved to dance, but I couldn't bear to think about it or watch anyone else dance after she was gone."

"Well, your majesty, your daughters have found another place to dance."

And the soldier told the king about the beautiful princesses' nightly adventures.

When the soldier had finished, the king replied, "It's an incredible story you've just told me. But do you really expect me to believe it?"

"Not without proof, your majesty," the soldier agreed, and he handed the king the branches from the silver, gold, and diamond trees.

The king turned the branches over several times and inspected them carefully. He knew these branches could not have been made by any of the craftsmen in his kingdom, and so he asked, "Do you have anything else to show me?"

"Yes," the soldier replied, and he drew from his pocket the embroidered napkin and the golden cup from the secret castle where the king's daughters danced each night away.

The stitching on the cloth was so unusual, and the cup was so light and beautiful. Both were unlike anything the king had ever seen. He summoned the princesses and asked them, "Well, daughters, is this true?"

The eldest princess looked thoughtfully at the soldier and then replied, "Yes, it is, Father. It's exactly as the soldier said. Oh, Father, we know you said we could not dance, but we couldn't help ourselves. Please forgive us. Our souls just wouldn't be still until they had their fill of dancing."

"Ah, dear daughter, there is nothing to forgive. It is I who should beg your pardon!" the king replied, his eyes filled with happy tears. Then he looked at the soldier and said, "You have found the answer to my question. Which of the princesses do you choose for your bride?"

Your eldest daughter," the soldier replied, "if she will have a man like me for a husband."

The eldest princess had become quite fond of the kind soldier. He had seen the world and was full of stories and jokes, and she had to admit that he was a very good dancer. And so she happily agreed.

The following week, the princess and the soldier were married. All the bells in the kingdom rang out, and the celebration went on all night. The remaining princesses invited the princes who had rowed them to the balls at the magic castle each evening, and soon these princesses were married as well. There was great joy in the kingdom for many years. And the cobblers were kept even busier than before, because now the whole kingdom danced and danced and danced.

About the Story

The earliest printed versions of "The Twelve Dancing Princesses" appeared in the 1800s with the collections of the Brothers Grimm, but pieces of this story have been a part of western mythology, folklore, and fairy tales for thousands of years. As fairy tale and myth scholars have pointed out, some of our earliest stories contain an account of the hero, like the soldier in this story, making a journey into the underworld. In the ancient Sumerian tale *The Epic of Gilgamesh* the hero enters the underworld to find the secret of immortality. In Greek mythology, Orpheus descends into the realms of the dead in the hope of bringing back his wife, Eurydice; Demeter goes there in search of her daughter, Persephone, who has been abducted by the god of the underworld, Hades; and the trickster hero Odysseus travels to these twilight places to learn his fate from the prophet Teiresias. In some of these journeys, the hero must cross a river or other body of water with the help of a ferryman. Often the hero brings back tokens from the underworld to prove that he has, in fact, been there. Like the soldier in "The Twelve Dancing Princesses," the young king Gilgamesh even finds trees covered with precious jewels when he travels to the land of the dead.

In fairy lore, there are plenty of dances and balls held underground, in fairy mounds, or in fields and forest clearings. Humans, however, are generally not invited to or welcome at these nightly festivities. Any mortal who visits them does so at his own peril. Indeed, it is said that if one enters the ring where the fairies are dancing uninvited, all sorts of enchantments may occur. Years can fly by in what seems to be only seconds and, at the end of the dance, the intruder may find himself much, much older than when he began.

"The Twelve Dancing Princesses" has taken various turns and twirls in its history as a fairy tale. It has traveled to the Punjab of India where there exists a version of the story called "Dorani," about a princess and her friend from the fairy realms who mysteriously disappear every evening on a flying stool to dance in the heavenly palace of Indra. Her young husband, eager to know where she goes, follows her, having been made invisible by a magic powder. And in an English tale called "Kate Crackernuts," a young woman agrees to watch over a sick prince during the night. But instead of being bed-ridden, he secretly goes dancing every evening inside a fairy hill, until the resourceful Kate finds a way to remove the spell that has been placed upon him. Clearly, there's a lot to be said in fairy tales for keeping your dancing shoes close by, and more importantly, for always staying light on your feet.

—J. C.

For the Muse, Terpsichore, and all those enthralled by her spirit in the great mystery of the Dance.   –J. C.

STERLING and the distinctive Sterling logo are registered trademarks of Sterling Publishing Co., Inc.

Library of Congress Cataloging-in-Publication Data Available

10 9 8 7 6 5 4 3 2 1

Published by Sterling Publishing Co., Inc.
387 Park Avenue South, New York, NY 10016
Text © 2009 by John Cech
Illustrations © 2009 by Lucy Corvino
The illustrations in this book were created using acrylic paints, inks,
watercolor, and pencil on watercolor board.
Distributed in Canada by Sterling Publishing
c/o Canadian Manda Group, 165 Dufferin Street
Toronto, Ontario, Canada M6K 3H6
Distributed in the United Kingdom by GMC Distribution Services
Castle Place, 166 High Street, Lewes, East Sussex, England BN7 1XU
Distributed in Australia by Capricorn Link (Australia) Pty. Ltd.
P.O. Box 704, Windsor, NSW 2756, Australia

Printed in China

Sterling ISBN 978-1-4027-4435-8

For information about custom editions, special sales, premium and corporate purchases,
please contact Sterling Special Sales Department at 800-805-5489 or specialsales@sterlingpublishing.com.